To Max Cohen Osher
and his cousins,
Charlotte Maya Kramer-Cohen
and
Lucas Gordon Kantrowitz
—M.E.

To my dad, mom,
brother, sister,
and Jen
—C.S.

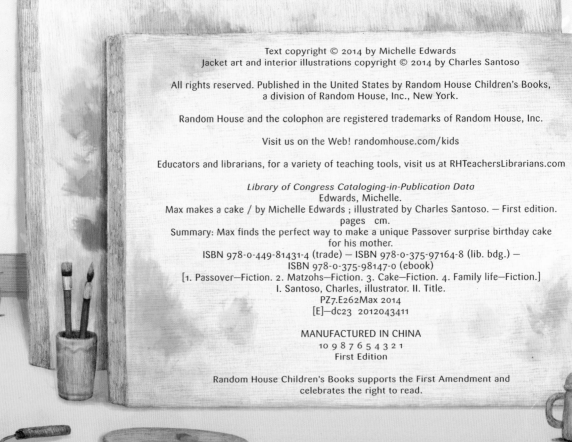

Text copyright © 2014 by Michelle Edwards
Jacket art and interior illustrations copyright © 2014 by Charles Santoso

Visit us on the Web! randomhouse.com/kids

Educators and librarians, for a variety of teaching tools, visit us at RHTeachersLibrarians.com

Library of Congress Cataloging-in-Publication Data
Edwards, Michelle.
Max makes a cake / by Michelle Edwards ; illustrated by Charles Santoso. — First edition.
pages   cm.
Summary: Max finds the perfect way to make a unique Passover surprise birthday cake
for his mother.
ISBN 978-0-449-81431-4 (trade) — ISBN 978-0-375-97164-8 (lib. bdg.) —
ISBN 978-0-375-98147-0 (ebook)
[1. Passover—Fiction. 2. Matzohs—Fiction. 3. Cake—Fiction. 4. Family life—Fiction.]
I. Santoso, Charles, illustrator. II. Title.
PZ7.E262Max 2014
[E]—dc23 2012043411

MANUFACTURED IN CHINA
10 9 8 7 6 5 4 3 2 1
First Edition

MAX
Makes a Cake

by **Michelle Edwards**
illustrated by **Charles Santoso**

Random House 🏠 **New York**

Max Osher was an expert at getting dressed.

He could almost tie his shoes.

And he knew the Four Questions for Passover in Hebrew and English. The other night, he sang them in both languages at the Passover Seder. All by himself. Without any help. The youngest child is supposed to ask them, but Max's sister, Trudy, was a baby. She couldn't even talk yet.

"When you're bigger, you'll have to know the Four Questions for Passover," Max told Trudy. "Why is this night different from all other nights? That's the first one.

"Because on this night, we eat matzoh. That's the answer," said Max. He spooned some smooshed banana right into Trudy's mouth.

"And you'll have to know the Passover story, too.

"A long time ago, the Jews were slaves in Egypt. When
Pharaoh freed them, they had to *hurry, hurry, hurry* away
with their bread on their backs. The sun baked it flat like
crackers. That's what matzoh is.

"Drink up. I have a cake to make."

Trudy tipped over her sippy cup. She spit out her banana smush. Then she pooped.

"Nap time," said Max.

Daddy took Trudy out of her high chair. "I'll be right back," he said.

"Hurry," said Max. "We have a cake to make."

It was Mama's birthday. She was downstairs working in her studio.

While Trudy napped, Max and Daddy were going to make a surprise birthday cake. They'd bought a special Passover cake mix at the supermarket.

"We are going to make a cake," sang Max. "A Passover cake. A birthday cake. A happy-birthday-for-Mama cake."

Max sang his song again. Was Daddy *still* changing Trudy's diaper? Why didn't he *hurry up*?

Max took a sip of milk from
Trudy's cup. All was quiet.

Trudy's door clicked shut.
The upstairs hallway creaked
with Daddy's footsteps.

"Cake time," said Max.

"Waah! Waah! Waah!" Trudy cried.

Daddy went back to her room.

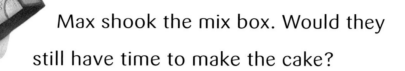

Max shook the mix box. Would they still have time to make the cake?

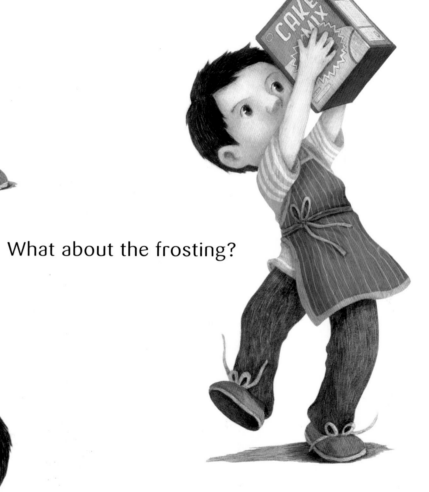

What about the frosting?

They hadn't bought a mix for that. A birthday cake had to have frosting!

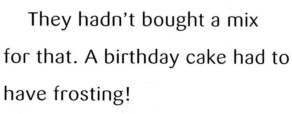

Max went to the refrigerator
and found some cream cheese
and red jam.

He stirred them together. He tasted a fingerful. *Yummy*. It was sweet and pink like frosting. *Very good*. So he made some more.

Now Max and Daddy needed to *hurry, hurry, hurry* to surprise Mama. But Daddy wasn't hurrying at all. What if Mama came upstairs before the cake was done?

"Waah!

Waah!

Waah!"

What if Daddy was busy with Trudy all afternoon?

"I don't want to wait anymore," said Max. "I want to make Mama's cake right now."

He smeared his frosting on a piece of
matzoh. Then, before he took even one bite . . .

Max had an idea.

Now all Max needed was a candle. And just as Daddy came in with baby Trudy, he found one.

"Ta-da!" said Max.

"Wow, Max," said Daddy. "You did
a terrific job!"

"Gurgle, gurgle, goo," said Trudy.

"Let's march to Mama right now," said
Max. And he led the cake parade, singing
"Happy Birthday" all the way.

Daddy lit the candle. Mama made a wish and blew it out.

Max sang "Happy Birthday" again. Then he sang the Four

Questions in Hebrew and in English.

"Want to know why this cake is different from all other cakes?" asked Max. "Because it's a *hurry, hurry, hurry* Passover cake. And I made it all by myself!"

How to Make a *Hurry, Hurry, Hurry* Cake

1. Mix some cream cheese and jam together.

2. Taste a fingerful, and add more jam
   if it's not sweet enough.

3. Then spread the frosting on a matzoh.

4. Top with another matzoh.

5. Add more frosting and more matzohs
   until your cake is just right for you.

The Four Questions for Passover

At the Seder, a special Passover meal, the youngest child asks the Four Questions. The answers help tell the story of Passover.

The Passover Story

Once, the Jews were slaves in Egypt. Their leader, Moses, said to Pharaoh, "Let my people go." Pharaoh said, "You can go." But then he changed his mind. This happened many times. The last time, the Jewish people hurried out of Egypt. They hurried so fast that the bread they took with them didn't have time to puff up. This flat bread was called matzoh. On Passover, Jews eat matzoh to remember when they were slaves in Egypt, and the thin, hard bread they ate as they journeyed to freedom.